Descending

White Death

Mountain

J. J. Bartel

This book is appropriate for ages thirteen and older.

Editing and formatting by KarolynEditsBooks.com

Cover art by George Patsouras

eBook ISBN: 979-8-9913762-2-8

Paperback ISBN: 979-8-9913762-4-2

Library of Congress Control Number: 2025928214

Bartel, J. J.

Descending White Death Mountain

Summary: On Frostfire Asteroid 12, Chaha must brave the weather, plants, and animals of the mountain to deliver medicine to the people below or they will certainly perish.

Acknowledgments

I am deeply grateful to Nepalese colleagues and friends who worked alongside me during my master's studies.

To Nikki and the rest of the beta readers who wanted to remain anonymous: Thank you for your insight.

Contents

Prologue

In a place where the Waters of Wisdom freeze, the ice moved like water. Fanatic Fires burned—not hot, but frozen cold—right beside the solid waters. This area between time and space was home to those who grow stories and invaded by those who twist stories.

One such twister of stories was a demon with intangible hatred that could touch and twists stories into nothing.

It tugged at a spot where snow and embers were fused. Touching it, the fire-flake expanded, and a massive mountain in space was displayed in the air. The twister released an indescribable corrupting power. It simulated the experience of hearing that your best friend was dead. It replicated the dread of knowing that whatever came next would never be as good as before. Such death and dread were coming for an entire mountain in a spot of time and space.

A new voice, not of words, but a rush of heat, beeped and twitched. Glassy lava, moving as a contraption, latched onto ice embers and sputtered. The mountain shrunk to a snowflake.

"Discovered already?" said the demon. "No matter. It does not matter what you blobs do. We demons are perfect at making things what they are meant to be: Dead. Still. Gone. Do you seriously think you can stop it?"

The glassy lava, jerking like a robot, emitted a thousand beeps that formed like words. "Your flow here. Limited. Energy. Once gone, banished."

The demonic presence without a face smiled. "Perhaps, but I can collapse worlds and galaxies. If you let me blow this one away, will there be less for you to protect? You could save the most important heroes then." The demon knew that a younger goop could be tempted.

The beeps turned to scraping and cracking glass. "No story dead. All. Necessary. Death one, death all."

The faceless cold wind scowled. "Those are words of an elder goop. Well, what did I expect from an elder goop? Reason? Prioritization?" The twisting demon's hatred expanded rapidly, making the Elder Glass Lava Goop seem small.

Yet it stayed latched onto the fragment. From its essence and being, beeps and glass-cracking sounds gave way to a pulse, radiating outward like a sphere, infusing itself into countless bits of frozen wisdom, cold fire, and snowflakes made of embers. Now these things along with the fragment were protected by red, semi-transparent glass lava boxes.

"Oh, you think you can protect all of these stories, all this folklore, from me? I bring forth the frostbite winds, and I will rend asunder all to nothing as it should be!"

A new sound, like sticky boiling honey and hissing and bubbling, almost delighted came from the goop. "Evil. Choice and existence. Theirs. Not yours to force. Neither mine. To fix."

The beeping, scraping, and bubbling went silent. Its form then cascaded into dread and death, glassy fire smoldering the demon. The demon could not scream for it had no mouth, but it threw a tantrum, blasting back cold winds, solidifying the outer layer of the goop and turning the transparent liquid lava into solid, dead, opaque glass. It cracked, shattered, and fell off.

Now less of both the demon and the Glass Lava Goop existed. This process would continue until one lost their presence entirely. Until one could save or destroy.

First Step Down

CHAHA

I was not allowed to be with family, friends, or even the khana.

Instead, I put a stylus to the desk screen and wrote, "My teachers tell me no child leaves the compound, the mountain, or the asteroid alone. None that survive, anyway. The elders are quick to say to all of us that Terra's mountains are adept at killing us."

I put the stylus down and stretched in my seat. My classmates have already left for the afternoon rest, but I had to do extra work: a written report on the history of this large prison.

It's even worse at Frostfire Asteroid 12. The only reason anyone stays here is because this place is one of thirty-three places where frostfire is mined and used for building spaceships. People come here, work for ten years, and make their dreams come true.

"I wish that were true. I'm twelve, and they still won't let me leave. They won't let me go with the Beard people," I said out loud.

I looked at my desk, scratched up with evidence of bullying, insults faintly visible even after washing most of it away. The top left edge was still a bit sticky from the gum her classmate spat there. The teachers and the elders do tell the students not to bully others. But no one gets into real trouble for it. Sometimes when the elders or teachers think they are alone, they call me a scoundrel, like they call the Beards. Talking privately did not stop rumors from flying about like snowflakes in a blizzard.

"Not like anyone would miss me anyway. Teachers, sisters, elders, and classmates won't let me ride the train down. Walking is impossible," I muttered.

I stared at the desk and the assignment for a moment longer before I forced myself to look out the windows. Some of my classmates were already dressed in casual clothes, a vibrant whirlwind of color. Eight of them were in a snowball fight, calling forth snowballs from thin air into their hands.

Meanwhile, I'm still in the uniform—light blue and white with no decorative fringes on the sleeves. You get fringes for magic. While everyone else who traveled here learns in a year how to make ice come out of their hands, I have been here my whole life and not even a snowflake. That's why the rumors spread. The gossip grows. Red paint gets flicked on my clothes in art class.

The only real comfort I experienced was during the time I spent with the Beards. Leader Beard, Second Beard, Sniffing Beard, Doctor Beard, and many more. They dressed in brilliant colors—scarlets and violets, oranges and yellows—brighter than the sun. Leader Beard, in particular, treated me well. Sometimes they were called men, other times scoundrels. I know their friends because they gave me candy and listened to my stories. They shared some of theirs with me. Sniffing Beard spoke of animals that I only heard in the middle of the night but never saw in person. Doctor Beard showed me plants that I had never seen before. They talked of how sometimes in the morning, instead of thick snow, dew would be on the ground. I'd never seen that before. Liquid water on the ground? Sometimes they talked about fighting fantastic beasts, but those stories always scared me, so they didn't tell them often.

Over the years, we became friends, more so than with any of the girls or women here. The main one, Leader Beard, says that soon we will go to the stars and will have a wonderful time. He says I just need to sit and wait and then I will see such wonderful things and have so much fun that all of this will be worth it. They promised to come at least once every month.

"So why is it almost three months since the last time?" I had to sigh. "Blizzards didn't stop you before, so why now?"

I wrote some more before turning the work in for the night. Tomorrow, there was going to be math, and how to measure distance with our hands and feet. To get a head start, I wanted to walk by the classroom where the teacher normally writes some notes for the next day before getting a meal. No one could get good food if they're at the back of the cafeteria line, especially during khana.

But on the way, I passed the talking room. We were not allowed to have personal talking boxes but could enter the room and talk to everyone. Not just to someone in the valley but someone among the stars, too.

A Beard was shouting on the other end of a call. I recognized the voice of Second Beard, who was either second in command or second in cookie, I still didn't know. Their constant teasing felt warm, almost like friendship.

Second Beard said, "The sickness is getting bad. Something new is in the ice—either something you're dumping or something that was always there. But it's making us sick. Whatever ice magic is going on, it's killing us. Three are dead. Half of the entire base is about to die!"

The older elder who was in the talking room replied, "If you scoundrels gave us the monthly metal, we could afford to spend extra money on healing pod fluids. We had to spend it on trying to repair the transporters on our side. The elder has requested me to tell you to stop calling. Shiver-blight is a fake disease, and making up a disease to excuse your crew's destructive behaviors is a second low." She disconnected the call with the bearded one and walked past me.

My mind was reeling. *Are my friends in trouble?* I wondered.

I could barely eat that night. I forced myself to swallow the roasted goat and veggies, because they would punish me if at least half the plate is not consumed.

Will they be happy? Are the Beards safe?

The worrisome night turned sour after Leader Beard came alone, rattling the outer-most fence, screaming, "Let us live, Granny, let us live!"

Two teachers escorted him inside. Following from a distance, I could hear angry voices, which is never a sign of a good meeting. Leader Beard was not just angry. I could hear fear in his shouting. This Beard had brought me candy, listened to my stories, and told me stories of life. He was the one who would take me away from this compound.

I felt both scared and angry for Leader Beard. It sounded like no one would help. That's when I decided. For the first time in a long time, I stood up straight, the top of my head barely reaching past my classmates' noses. I went to the nurses' office, where the healing pods were. I saw the molten red fluids in the tubes that were no bigger than my hand. One full tube could reattach limbs and waken the sleeping. I took several, as many as I could fit in my uniform pockets. I also managed to find a tent box. Then I quietly made my way to my room to get some cold-weather gear from my locker. I dressed as warmly as I could, with thinning gloves, the thickest boots that I could never grow into, and even two blankets. While everyone else was attending an afternoon fun activity of their choosing, I chose a rescue mission. No one noticed me leaving through one of the side doors.

I set off to descend White Death Mountain.

Second Step Down

CHAHA

I went beyond the compound's fence, wearing oversized boots, a patchy coat, thinning gloves, and a backpack of hot medicine. The fence gates wouldn't open for me, so I had to approach the black barbed fence. There was a spot where the barbs were only as long as a fingernail instead of a finger. I took the thicker blanket and threw it up and over, the barbs catching on the cloth.

The patchy gloves with holes that I wore meant that climbing twice my height was not easy, especially with the heavy backpack. Looking down from the top of the fence, I could feel my confidence waver. Keeping balance was hard because the wind was stronger this high up, threatening to toss me onto the rocks and crusted snow. *I don't know if I can do this, but I have to. They didn't have a choice.*

I slowly turned around to begin the climb down. The fence was covered in thorns, barbs, and other sharp points to discourage anyone from climbing. A sudden gust of wind hit my face, and snowflakes went up my nose. The cold tickle made me sneeze, which sent me tumbling off the fence. I grabbed the blanket, and it tore in two, causing me to land on my back with a loud crack.

The medicine! I threw off the pack and unzipped the big pouch. Small test tubes filled with warm reddish-orange liquid radiated heat, warming my face. No cracks in the glass. Good. Then, out of the corner of my vision, I spied broken vines and thorns sprinkled with wet blood, already freezing to the unforgiving fence. My arm had a nasty-looking scratch.

That's my blood! The sight of it made me cry out. Covering my mouth in time, my reflexive scream was quieter than the wind. Couldn't get caught now. The realization made me shiver, not just from the cold.

I slapped a pocket bandage over the wound, tightened the jacket, and now it was time. Carrying the pack of scarlet tubes radiating heat, I was about to move when I heard a Beard scream.

LEADER BEARD

Earlier that day, I—the one Chaha calls Leader Beard—was escorted into the compound, a cool gray brick building with off-white mortar that made it look frostbitten.

The two teachers guided me to one of the administrative rooms, where the matriarch, who I called Granny, waited. She was the leader, the boss of the entire compound. She had light brown skin and wore a dark-blue long-sleeved shirt with embroidery covering every little bit. I saw ice, wind, snow, real and mythical animals, and even geometric patterns on the thick shirt and flowing black dress. I stared hard.

She barely paid me—with my somewhat darker copper-colored skin, plain and rough clothing, and an even harsher face—any mind.

We must have this conversation. So, I took a deep breath and tried again for the fourth time. "You are condemning us to death. And you needed to be reminded of that. Just because your people don't die from the cold doesn't mean we don't."

"It'll be a problem for us if too many of you die. That'll increase our workload," Granny said.

I felt my fist slam the table before I realized my intention, fury flushing my face, and shouted, "These are people! They may not be special in the way you're used to thinking of people, but they are still people who don't deserve to die."

"I don't get to choose any of your weaknesses. We all signed waivers to come here. We all know the risks when we get the injections. And now that one of the risks has become reality, you want to break the contract?"

"You can choose to send a few maidens down the rail so that we can stop dying. You can spare two elders, even two teachers. We need the medicine, and your previous shipments have not gone through," I said.

"It's not my fault that you cannot manage the communications or connections. We had automatic transport until you scoundrels broke it in your riots," Granny said, narrowing her graying eyebrows at him.

I felt my hands clench from the conversation. With great effort to keep my tone civil, I replied, "The transport was supposed to be used for equivalent exchange. We mine the metal. Then we send it to you women to use your weird ice powers on the metal, sell it to that spaceship company for top dollar, and we all make a profit. For years now, you have been making up problems and docking our pay through contract loopholes. We are no longer eating half the goat. You give us burnt skin while you eat the whole goat!"

She rolled her eyes in frustration, shooing him away with her hands. "Are we just going to keep going back and forth, or are you going to go back to the visitor room?"

"We agreed to work here for the contract for a mountain of money at the end. We haven't received half of what we were supposed to. You've made it impossible for us to buy the medicine from other places!" I accused.

"We're literally the twelfth asteroid of thirty-three that now sell this material. There's competition. We are both poorer than desired."

"You mean competition for how much you can skim off the top?"

There was a loud, furious knocking on the other side of the wooden door. Judging by the sound, it was by a woman and could not be ignored.

Granny sighed. "This day keeps getting better and better. Come in!"

A woman stumbled into the room. A younger lady with embroidery from the fringe to the elbows of her garment said with a flushed face, "There's a problem, Grand Elder!"

"It couldn't wait until tomorrow?"

"When we double-checked the beds, Chaha was missing. Not only that, but some of the medicine is also gone!"

Granny might not care, but I did. Bolting out of the room down the winding off-white corridors with their sky-blue decorations, student achievements, and faculty notices, I came to the big cedar doors. Kicking them open allowed me to dash into the courtyard without breaking my stride.

"Chaha, Chaha, where are you??" I yelled.

Granny and the woman were struggling to keep up with me as they were walking. I turned left and started running around searching for a child too small for this imposing place. My child. The last flesh, face, and blood of my love. She was most likely out here in this courtyard somewhere. I had to look everywhere, find footprints, anything. If she'd been chased up a tree or was crying in a corner somewhere, I must be there for her.

CHAHA

I heard Leader Beard screaming my name, and looking back, I felt tears forming. What I wanted to do was turn back and cry in that soft beard. What they needed was for me to start walking down. Rubbing my face, not wanting liquid to freeze on my skin, I had to keep walking.

When I was alone, you were there. Now you're alone. Let me do the same for you.

Third Step Down

LEADER BEARD

Back at the gray building, after an hour of searching, I finally spotted the torn blanket stuck in the barbs on the fence.

"That's Chaha's!" Sprinting to the fence, I saw red streaks of her blood and her torn blanket, marking her struggle to cross the barbed wire. "My Chaha is hurt."

Granny and the teacher managed to follow me everywhere I went.

Under her breath, Granny spoke our language, Nepalese, but with a blizzard's chill. "Pānī ra batāsakō sātha, rahanuhōs."

I was stuck. I looked down to see blue and purple ropes made of woven snowflakes wrapped around me, covering my body from my ankles to my mouth.

"Hotheads," Granny said. "Getting themselves killed for stupid reasons. Even you will die in this night air without a good jacket." She turned to the teacher and said, "Hey, you, he's trapped now. I will let security know that if Chaha knocks at the gate, she is to be let in, no matter what. Put *him* in the guest room. He can be stupid in the morning."

How dare she? How dare she neglect her! I thought, fury rising, a molten fire, red and orange liquid, radiating from my body. The ice hissed at the heat before cracking and shattering. "I'm getting my jacket and leaving now!" I said angrily.

Granny just pointed at me with eyes that glowed blue and purple. "Pānī ra batāsakō sātha, ēka kama uṭhnuhōs."

Water and wind twisted about from the ground, encasing me in a clear prison like a cramped, human-sized goat carrier. It was several fingers thick, and I was not getting out of it. Granny rolled her eyes at me and started walking away.

The teacher said, "I am sorry about this. The weather forecast is brutal. A blizzard, with wind so strong it might pick up ice, rock, or even trees, is what's expected. The drones won't go far, but if she is nearby, they can find her."

Then she whispered some words, and a little snowwoman no bigger than a shoe was formed. She waved it inside, and it picked up my prison and carried me into a guestroom. She left me in the bathroom, and when she closed the door, the glass shattered, leaving me trapped as a guest.

I ripped the purple-blue ice from my body. Sprinting to the door, I banged on it again and again, screaming my daughter's name. But the door was reinforced. I could not even dent the metal, let alone break free. The basic hotel room had no windows. I dropped into the soft chair, its warmth mocking me for what Chaha must be going through.

"What if she meets a Chyangra? The wild ones grow twice as big as the tame ones and are not used to humans. They have horns curved to sharp points, are stubborn and aggressive, walk silently on top of snow and rock, and sleep in snowbanks. Stumbling into one is bad. Even a glancing blow can kill a man. She-" The thought horrified me, a tear flowing down my cheek. "Short-faced bears, saber-toothed tigers... so many things can go wrong. Where are you?"

CHAHA

I fought the urge to cry as I started walking, one step at a time. That's how Doctor Beard always told me to deal with hard things. One step, one sip of medicine, one shot, one bean. Gross. After countless steps, I began to pay more attention to the mountain. On this part of the mountain, the trees could not grow tall, which allowed me to see several miles or kilometers down the slope. Beards used miles, and teachers used kilometers.

Some moments were still, but in others, the wind picked up the loose snow, and I had to look down in front of me to see the path. My legs are small, and in these boots, slipping would be easy, so watching out for patches of ice was a must. A tumble here would mean falling a great distance and then dying on impact.

For over an hour, I stepped this way, making my way down. The snow obscured my vision of what was ahead of me and what I had left behind.

I wish the rail worked. This mountain path was close enough to the road. So, I was hidden. And right now, that's what mattered.

A surprise gust flung snow in my face, and I stumbled back. Instead of gripping rock, the boot slipped on ice, and I could feel myself falling. Reaching out, I tried to grab something, but gravity wanted to fling me down.

As I started to fall, the world seemed to slow down, and a memory from the Beards came to me.

After giving me some cheese and a doll, Sniffing Beard had said quietly, "It's easy to fall and hurt yourself. White Death Mountain has a way of killing people. If you feel like you're falling, tuck together. Bring your legs close, cover your neck with one arm, and your face with the other. A tight pebble hurts less than a stretched-out noodle on the mountain." He sniffed his cheese, smiled and bit into the block.

As soon as the memory hit, I curled up right away and did not fall far.

"Thank the Beards," I muttered. Their memories always seemed to come when they were needed.

The fast fall ended with a hard stop, hitting hair and muscle. My world spun with the sky meeting the ground. A mass of hair and muscle rose up. I wanted to give it space, but I could not move fast. I got lucky and bounced into a snow drift, so nothing immediately hurt. Whatever that was, I would have to confront it.

After it shook the snow off, I realized it was a wild Chyangra goat. Unlike some of the goats back at the compound that reached up to my chest in height, this one could look me in the eyes. The foreign black rectangular pupils and the light blue iris were unnerving, like a monster ready to pronounce judgment. Snorting and shaking, thick, wispy, white fur shook under its lean muscles. Hooves blacker than a moonless night stomped the ground.

I could feel every vibration jolting my entire body, rattling the medicine I was carrying. Its pale tan and white horns curved to a nasty point, looking more like a sharpened cudgel than bone from a beast.

I took a step back in fear, facing the man-killing goat. It lowered its head at me, ready to charge.

Fourth Step Down

The wild goat did not understand what humans were. Just that whatever was in front of her was not a goat; it was a not-goat. It hit her while she slept, so it was a threat. It was moving away but might try to strike again. She reared up on her hind legs, kicking hard with her black cloven feet, belting, "Ma-baa-baa!" over and over. Yet the creature did not run. So, the safest thing would be to lower her head and charge...

CHAHA

Fear gripped me as I stared at the wild Chyangra goat. Tall and heavy, it angrily snorted and bellowed, kicking the air at me, and then lowered its head to charge. Involuntarily, my feet dug into the ground, turning up snow and dirt, kicking and shoving myself back. I took a deep breath and tried to calm down.

Thinking about Beard wisdom, I wondered what they would do and felt a flicker of heat in my chest. As if summoned, a memory of Bald Quiet Beard struck me.

"Turn your body to the side. Wild goats. Stubborn and afraid. Everything eats them. Charge at sudden movements. Still and slow. Safe." Then he handed me some candied fruit.

If only I had not taken it then. A classmate's jealousy over candy was not to be underestimated.

I took a deep breath, inhaling a chill with snowflakes and froze. The sudden stillness made the goat freeze up. Slowly, I turned my head and saw steep slopes. Beyond the goat was a path, steeper than before, but the direct path to the trees below.

"How do I get past you?" I asked the goat, slowly moving away from her.

The female Chyangra froze when I did. Was it going to run? Was it going to strike again? I slowly started moving, not towards her but to the side. As I moved away, the goat noticed something and had to charge.

She seemed to be letting me go when she suddenly cried, "Baa-Ma!" and then jolted toward me. In fear, I tucked my legs to my chest, wrapped one arm around my knees and one around my face, and clenched. Any moment, I was sure I would get rammed.

Any moment now.

But it did not happen.

I felt something weird on my boot. Opening my eyes slowly, I saw the goat nibbling on my boot with worn teeth; no, it was munching on some black and green moss stuck to my boot. It gave my boot one final lick before moving over to eat more black-green moss nearby. It stared at me but seemed to be relaxed.

I backed away slowly, from my bent position, using my hands and feet. It flicked its thick ears at me, dismissing me with the gesture. Carefully, I got up and walked away from the goat and did not feel the tension melting away until I reached the trees.

Ducking behind the first tree, I muttered to myself, "I'm alive! That was too close. The forest seems safer. Okay, okay. What's Leader Beard always telling me? Right. Take a deep breath and think. Okay." I took a deep breath in, then pushed it out after several seconds. "The road is to my left." I breathed on my hands, my fingertips chilled, hope warming my heart. "The tree line is a quarter of the way down the mountain. I might be able to make it if I don't stop walking."

I then carefully wove between the many trees. Because of how high up the mountain they were, the few trees that could grow there were small, stunted, bent, and warped from the surrounding environment. I had to step between withered rhododendrons, bent junipers, damaged deodar cedars, broken chir pines, sad-looking blue pines, and stunted morinda spruces. I had only seen them in books before, and now I was touching their leaves, bark, and branches. Rough yet beautiful in their own way.

Being out here was far different from the lifeless, cold halls with classmates and the ever-watching teachers and elders. There were some pruned trees in the courtyard, but this steep mountainside was covered in dense natural forest. For the first time, I touched the trees beyond the fence.

One stood out to me from a distance. The deodar cedar, with its short, stumpy pine needles, has a sky-blue tinge. My fingers touched the streaky brown and pale-blue bark. Rough. Woody. Alive. Looking down, I saw a wound bleeding and oozing golden-hued sap from the only branch with new buds on the entire tree.

"You're wounded," I said. Upon closer inspection, I could see that the broken branch was barely attached by small, stubborn fibers.

Grabbing the dangling branch, I tried to put it back, whispering, "You can do it. You can make it." For several minutes, I stood there in the cold, holding the branch in place, watching the sap slowly ooze out all over the wound. They had given me books about life around here, and this should work. But what's in a book was not always true. I hadn't seen any dragonflies around here, and I was scared to ask about unicorns. Or mothers.

When the cold started to harden the sap, I let out a breath I did not realize I was holding in. "You did it. We can make it." Like the sap, a golden, radiant smile flowed on my face. I hugged myself to warm up, then to be comforted. My fingers brushed against the scars on my arm.

For a brief moment, the bitter disagreement that had led to those scars flashed through my mind. My classmates had tried to steal the cheese and candy, and I wanted to get it back. One of them had snapped her fingers, causing an ice shard to fly too fast and cut too deep, leaving behind a streak in her flesh.

"We can make it," I said to the tree. The Beards had taught me to bandage wounds, make poultices, and which sap would make the best tea. They'd cried over my injury more than I did that day. "Well, we can if we get a little help," I added. I continued walking again—grinning—down the mountainside.

LEADER BEARD

On top of the mountain, I resigned myself to the room. The fridge had some bottled water, and I downed one after another, wishing it were something more substantial. Maybe then the thoughts would not hit me so hard.

I hope Chaha is okay. I don't know if I could forgive you, Granny, if we can't find her. Don't you realize who you are hurting?

I could also imagine Granny's response: "You wonder if you could forgive? You wonder? That's rich coming from you, Head Patriarch! The blizzard is coming, and if that fool of a thing does not turn around to the drones, that's her fault!"

I groaned in the chair, stress catching up to me, giving me one last thought before I started to sleep. *I hope she turns back before reaching the forest.* If the never-ending winter did not kill her, the animals would, and the caves. Falling into one of those was so easy. There was always something on White Death Mountain searching for new lives to take.

Fifth Step Down

CHAHA

Night descended, forcing those who walked by day to sleep. The people could not wait for me to sleep while they were sick. Yet the mountain took no prisoners—only lives. I know I am twelve and small for my age, and if the Beards can freeze in hours, I will probably freeze in minutes. So, I needed to find a flat part of the land, flat enough for a camp, while I still had daylight.

Minutes before the sun sank below the horizon, I finally found a small, flat part of land that would work. I set my bag down and scrambled to check the red medicine, which radiated warmth. I discovered a small crack on one of the bottles, which did not calm me down. It was not a deep crack, so nothing was leaking. Good.

Breathing a sigh of relief, I kept searching my bag for a small, firm black box. Putting it on the ground, I pressed the top button for five seconds and said, "Release home." The box then began beeping, and I gave it space. What was once no larger than my hands quickly expanded, filling with air. The thin, black yet sturdy tarp came to a point at the top, and a pyramid-like tent with a flat top was formed in less than a minute.

"It's so huge! And these are the smalls? It's bigger than my bed!" I exclaimed. I went to the narrow end facing me and grabbed the zipper-like sealer, opening up the tent.

Inside, it was dark blue, with darker blue lines outlining the door. Zipping the tent shut, for the first time today, I was free from the wind's tricks. Taking off my pack, I explored the inside, feeling the material with my fingers. "Amazing," I whispered.

Exhaustion would not let me stay awake for long. I took off my boots, grabbed the torn blanket, and tried to get warm. After lying down, I found a rectangular patch with light-blue buttons and lettering. The words were so worn that they could barely be read, but I pressed one of the buttons. The tent top came alive, becoming transparent, and now I could see the trees and the hundreds of shimmering stars through the tent. Despite the events of the day, such a sight made me relax, and I felt a bit warmer. Soon, a memory from years ago came back to me.

"There's a great and mighty story in these stars. Way over there," Leader Beard had said, pointing northward to a cluster of stars, "is where humans once lived. Long ago, humans only lived on one planet. However, we have now expanded beyond that solar system. A man or a woman can go anywhere, work for ten years, and live well for the rest of their lives. It's hard work with no guarantee of survival, but I wouldn't trade this for anything. I meet good people, many friends, and family."

"Like Head Maiden?" I asked.

Everyone grew quiet, and Leader Beard, with a pained look on his face, said, "I was thinking of people like you."

It was my turn to stay quiet for a moment. Then I said, "They say my name means to want, and greed, and they call me a joke."

"Nepalese is a difficult language. Some might say want, but when you were named, Chaha meant loving wish. For me, you are a wish come true, and you always brought me joy and laughter every time I met with you." He then picked me up and pointed at some stars to the north. He said, "Many families live on the Star of Nepal. There we can sing, dance, eat, drink, and party every weekend. The rice fields are rich, momo dumplings abound all over the place, thukpa noodle soup flows like a river, and everyone can eat Sel Roti bread! It's almost sweeter than sunshine on your face! Since every day is good, we can eat the chatamari—spiced and seasoned—whenever we like."

He had turned to her in his embrace and said, "If you want, when you're fifteen, you will be an adult. My work term will end. We can go anywhere, and if you'd like, we can go together. Whaddaya say?"

"Let's go to New Nepal," I replied aloud in the present, exhaustion catching up to me and forcing me to sleep and dream. Snow and night fell.

The early light chased away the wind. Another day was starting, and the sunshine and gentle heat woke me. As much as I desired five more minutes, I caught a glimpse of the pack. So, I got up, dressed, carried my stuff out of the tent, then pressed a button, making the tent shrink down to a small box again. I put it in my pack and repeated the process of taking one step at a time.

"No wind, no snow. I might be able to make it down by the end of today," I mused. As I walked, the sun rose, and birds woke up. The hooting of owls going to bed had given way to cooing mourning doves, chirping babblers, shouting magpies, and whistling robins. *It's like the world is singing.* Occasionally, I closed my eyes and just let the sounds wash over me.

Before an hour had passed, I heard a frightful, piercing shriek off to my left, and turning, I saw three birds: one shimmering male and two drab females. They were heading straight for me. A massive cat with hunger in its eyes stalked behind them. Not a house cat. It was larger than me, the goat, and even the Beards.

Shocked, I started to move down the mountain faster, but my boots hit another icy spot and I tumbled. I tucked myself in and did not drop far, hitting a chir pine. I knocked some needles from its branches, and it knocked the wind out of me.

The predator's fur was white with black stripes. Its two huge upper front dagger-like teeth crunched through feathers and flesh. One of the birds was torn apart. It may have been a Monal Pheasant. Now it was a mess of shimmering orange, green, blue, indigo, and purple feathers, flying apart and stained with blood.

Now that the big cat was feeding, I took a good look, and a memory struck me as I started to run. My body seemed to heat up quickly, helping me to move faster, away from certain death. I cared not for any more ice, sprinting as I remembered what Leader Beard had told me about some of the animals.

"Chaha, while this is a mining place, all sorts of animals live here. Somehow, a living land makes more metal and ice. Somehow. The first people that came here did something to its core, and now the metal grows. They used science beyond my understanding. What I do understand is that one of the scariest animals here is the Siberian saber-toothed tiger. A cross between the Siberian Tiger and Albino saber-toothed tigers. One of the most dangerous animals above ground. Yes, above—the caves are far more dangerous."

Suddenly, the ground gave way, and I felt my body float for a moment before beginning to fall.

Sixth Step Down

CHARA

I tumbled away from the Siberian sabertooth. Spinning forward, I landed on my back and on top of the medicine. The snow cushioned my fall but did not prevent one of the most terrifying sounds I have ever heard. Not the sound of a pheasant being torn apart or the cries of the living going silent. I heard a crack.

Getting my bearings, I went to the edge of the cave area and hid in the shadows where I took off my backpack and looked inside. One of the vials was cracked and leaking fluid. As it was exposed to the air, it lost its red and orange glow and its cooling effect, turning dull, dirty brown. I tried to scoop it back in, but it just dirtied my hands. The cut I received during the fall stung, so I took some of the red and orange fluid and put it on the cut and some of my scrapes.

Putting the pack back on and really looking around, I noticed several tunnels that I could walk through. I had fallen too far to climb up, so I would enter the tunnels. The Beards say that if you can feel a breeze, you're close to the outside. So, I went to the left. I placed my hand on the left wall of the cave so that I didn't get turned around even if it became too dark to see.

Taking slow, steady steps, I began walking. Even as the darkness swallowed me, I could feel the wind getting stronger and stronger. At one point, I felt a breeze coming from two different directions, but following either would require me to take my hand off the wall, so I did not. Taking careful steps, I followed the tunnel around a curve, and before long, saw blue sky through an opening.

"Almost there. Just a bit more walking, and I will see the outside," I reassured myself. As I approached the opening, I realized that this was not a simple exit but a hole in a cliff. In the distance, I could see a vast expanse of forest and the best sight I could hope to see at the moment.

"Smoke!" I saw smoke up ahead. Doctor Beard would say that it's better to burn a bit of wood than freeze, so figured the power must be out. I felt that I must be getting so close. "But this drop..." Looking down, I saw a vine, covered in barbs and thorns, each one tipped with delicate blue. Creeping frostbite. One cut, and I would have to use one of the vials on me. But they needed every single vial.

My body felt a pain. I wanted to cry and weep at being so close and yet so far. I rubbed my face. I remembered feeling the breeze coming from another direction and decided to take my chances. Taking out one of the vials, which shone red and orange, I held it in front of me to light my way, tracing my way back through the cave until I felt the other breeze. Taking a risk, I followed the breeze to what I hoped was an exit I could actually use.

It was not to be.

As I walked deeper and deeper into the tunnel, I noticed the cracks and gaps far above me where the breeze was coming from. The walls were too smooth for me to climb, removing any chance I had of getting out that way.

But then I noticed a green glow not far in the distance. Having no other choice, I walked closer to it with the red-orange medicine lighting the way. In a little while, the tunnel widened into a massive room that took my breath away. I felt my whole body go slack with wonder at what I saw.

The cavern, barely taller than me, was covered with a neon-green glowing moss. It lit up the strange room, with various flowers covering the ground. The pale-pink rhododendrons were fragile. Stunted marigolds shimmered. Soft purple violets speckled with silver that seemed too weak to live thrived among the others.

The flowers and the light were but a part of the wonder. The butterflies were unlike any displayed in books the Beards had shown me. The mormons flitted about the rhododendrons, black bodies seemingly sucking in the light while their pink wings danced like flower petals in a breeze. Common brimstones, with their neon-green wings, blended well with the moss. Those in flight revealed their white underbellies like a star twinkling in the night sky.

"Beautiful," I breathed. As I walked around the room, butterflies came and landed on me for a moment, letting me see them up close. For a minute, I forgot about the bullying and the deadly trip down and sat down in this wonderful place and enjoyed being tickled by butterflies.

I did not notice the sloth until a fuzzy rock in the wall moved. The sloth was twice as tall as me, had dark-gray fur, and was covered in glowing green moss. Its dull yet rigid claws that were longer than a Beard's fingers scraped up flowers and moss for food. As it moved, I saw water dripping from a crack in the ceiling and forming a small pool.

They told me not to drink the snow because it would chill me too much. But I had no water, and who knows when or if I would reach the village. Sloths don't fight, they say. If I gave it space and walked around it, I might be able to drink.

Every step forward brought me closer to the animal and closer to the small pool of water. Each step disturbed the flowers and moss, causing neon lights to flicker on the walls. Finally, keeping some space between me and the sloth, I approached the pool on one side, while the animal remained on the other. Slowly, I knelt, cupped water in my bare hands, and sipped.

After a bit, I sat back, looking up to see that the sloth had quietly moved closer to me, and was patting me on my shoulder. The rugged, hairy arm reminded me of the strangers from beyond the mountain. The memories forced the tears to fall from my eyes, and I grabbed the sloth, sobbing in the moss-matted fur.

That's why I never saw the bear coming.

Seventh Step Down

LEADER BEARD

While Chaha was getting sloth hugs, I rose from slumber in the guestroom. This time the door was unlocked. When I swung it open, there was Granny, the matriarch.

"Granny, have the drones found anything?" I asked.

"You're too much before morning tea. No, they have not found any trace of her. And before you take off, I've frozen your pack and locked it up, and it won't thaw out until after breakfast. Due to a rare bit of luck, the blizzard seems to be delayed for a day. She is most likely alive so you can find her after breakfast. For now, we eat, scoundrel."

Granny walked off toward the smell of food that was growing by the minute. My stomach grumbled, so I followed her. We arrived at a great cafeteria. Girls and young women emerged and formed a line leading to a table with food piled upon it. A few women were dishing out food to others, while most were chatting with their peers, accepting the same bowls of food. The matriarch and the patriarch got a bowl of oats mixed with goat milk.

Farther down the line, Granny said, "The usual," thrusting out her bowl. The server nodded and gave her some soft dried figs with some dried gooseberries. With a snort and a barely perceivable nod, Granny accepted it and walked to the end of the table, skipping everything else but the drink.

I looked at the server—her nametag said Sarita. "What do you recommend?"

The maiden's eyes widened. "Sweet fruit is a hit with the kids, and the teens feel more mature having some hard nuts," she said.

I said, "I will avoid those and let them have it."

A glint of mischief shone in her eyes. "If you want to help us, the dried coconuts and apples are almost out. The matriarch says not to waste food, so we won't get a new shipment of mangoes, papayas, or apricots until the coconuts and apples are gone."

"Then please give me a double portion of coconuts and apples," I said with a smile. She took the bowl, and her eyes lit up when she felt the metal coin I slipped her underneath the bowl. "Think of that as my thanks. Not everyone has treated Chaha well."

The maiden pocketed the coin. "She's been through a lot, yet she smiled when your group visited. Stubborn like the matriarch," she said.

Grateful, I continued down the line, meeting up with Granny for drinks.

"You don't have my tea ready?" Granny asked the server.

"We ran out of White Silver yesterday. I just found out this morning because it's my first time serving this week," the server said.

"Next time you run out, send a note. Until that comes in, give me some black. Night Killer."

"The strong-"

"Considering how *he* will upend the morning," Granny interrupted, jabbing a thumb at me, "yes, I need the strongest cup."

The server, who was also the new teacher, gave her one of the mugs filled with hot water and a little tea pouch. Then, she went away to one of the far tables in a huff.

"Why wasn't I told?" Granny muttered under her breath. "The little scoundrel runs off, the big scoundrel complains, no one tells me about the tea, and everyone wonders why I have so many wrinkles."

"You were never one to open up about anything," I said, sitting next to her. "You're just like my wife. She would never share what was bothering her until it got to be too much."

"Don't speak of my daughter. And things change," she said, narrowing her eyes. "People always change and rarely for the better. Just look in the mirror."

"Even now, I think something good burns bright in-" I started.

"After my daughter died, the only fiery passion I have left is all the heartburn from stress. You two made sure that the good future is gone now."

I, the patriarch, and Granny, the matriarch, sat alone in silence. As we were finishing our food, the maiden I'd given a coin to before came over to the table.

"Madam, what of Chaha?" she asked.

Granny shrugged. "I don't know. I will unfreeze the door after breakfast, and he can search for her."

"Is there a chance she is still alive? What if she's in one of the caves?" the server asked.

"The caves would shelter her against the wind," I said, "but also expose her to some of the most dangerous animals on the mountain. Like in the butterfly caves."

"They sound beautiful," she said.

"Those sparkling death traps shelter great sloths and snow sloth bears. While the big, slow sloths are mostly harmless, the bears are dangerous. The sloths have ways to defend themselves, but the bears are always hungry. Modern firepower can kill one, but a man on his own would not survive an attack by one of those things," I said. "They can track bleeding prey up and down the mountain, ambushing from the caves. One minute you're alive, then teeth appear, then you're dead."

CHAHA

While the patriarch's hope silenced the table, I cried in the arms of a beast.

But not for long.

I felt my body being flung through the air, and my pack made a sharp cracking sound. My head was filled with stars and pain. As the world started spinning around, I could barely see the sloth. The bear was on top of it.

The bear's face was stained red with blood. The sloth tried to swipe its claws at the bear to defend itself, but the bear kept tearing out bits of flesh and bone. In a last-ditch attempt, the sloth shifted its legs and peed on the bear. Dark yellow fluid arced into its face, eyes and nose, and its furred flesh began to hiss and boil. The bear stumbled backward with an angry roar, and the sloth slowly escaped down the tunnel from which I'd come.

In desperation, I went down the other tunnel. There was no time for careful stepping, just a blind dash with my hand against the left wall. While the bear was distracted, I had to run, even as I kept running into walls and my gloves could not protect my hands from scrapes and cuts.

Suddenly, I heard a wet, throaty roar like something was trying to yell and gargle at the same time.

All I could think was, *No, no, no, no, no!*

Eighth Step Down

CHAHA

I had to stop believing my ears. The bear's roars echoed and sounded like they were both in front of and behind me. Maybe two bears were chasing me!

Fear and dwindling hope weakened my legs. Yet as I turned another corner, down the cavern, I saw light. As I raced for the light, lungs burning, a memory drifted into my mind.

"Mazes are tricky. One day, I will show some of these caves," Leader Beard said.

"Why?" I asked.

He handed her a small red candy ball. She put it into her mouth to discover strawberry, mango, and other flavors she had never tasted before. Her face showed everyone her joy, and everyone smiled to see her face.

"Like you, they can be beautiful, Chaha,"

Leader Beard said. "Some rooms have glowing moss and butterflies."

"Beautiful yet dangerous, Leader," Quiet Beard added. "Like so many other things. Lots of noise scares bears."

Leader Beard said, "It's more important to stay together. Getting separated is the most dangerous thing to do on the mountain. However, there is one upside to all these caves, Chaha. If someone keeps walking along the same wall of a tunnel long enough, they will eventually find a way out."

I repeated to myself in the present, "They will eventually find a way out..." Behind me, another roar, sounding drier, rose the hair on the back of my neck. I continued rushing down to the light without stopping.

As I got closer to the light, my heart lurched at the sight before me. There was a gap ahead, large enough for me and the pack to get through, but it was covered in a layer of ice. Thin enough to see the world on the other side, but thick enough to deny me access.

"I gotta try!" Grabbing a loose rock, I bashed

it against the ice, hit after hit, chip after chip, crack after crack, and yet the ice did not shatter. The scrapes and cracks only made the surface of the ice rough, and I could no longer clearly see through it.

"I have to help them, they help me," I said in a panicked voice. Grabbing a second rock, I swung it against the ice using both hands. My thoughts raced. *Every time I was cold, they warmed me. Even when the teachers and elders laughed at me, they helped.* The first rock slipped out of my hand, so I grabbed another and started pounding with it.

They made me laugh. They made me happy. Now they need help, and I'm going to help them. I just need to stay alive to get there.

Another impact forced me to look at my hands, fresh blood flowing from the fingers and palms in thin rivulets. I had not entirely broken through the ice yet, and the bear's thundering roar was getting closer to me.

I dropped to my knees, and whispered, "Am I gonna die?"

While Leader Beard left the compound, the teacher who he had given the coin to was flipping it between her fingers.

One of the teacher's friends burst through the door. "It's metal tempering practice. You coming?" she asked.

Sarita paused before grasping the coin and said, "No, I'll be late."

"One of the ancient hags is doing today's lesson. You can't risk-" her friend started to say.

"Leader gave me this, one of the old silver coins from Earth. Worth more than coppers or silver now. Just because we ignored the matriarch's request to ignore Chaha and called in an emergency search from the valley."

Her friend facepalmed, groaning. "You bleeding heart. Fine. For five coppers, I will tell that hag you got stomach cramps."

"Three?" Sarita countered.

"I am not risking punishment for three. Five."

"Four?"

Her friend sighed. "If I get it before supper, and if we don't get caught, I'll take four."

"Thank you, you're the best!" Sarita said, grabbing four copper coins and giving them to her, quickly running out the door.

She walked through many halls, past the cafeteria and the healing pods. She peeked around a few corners to avoid other adults. Bathrooms were great for hiding. Avoiding a few cameras, she made it to the far building.

After she knocked five times on a door panel, it opened. A pair of blue-purple eyes darted around and a voice said, "Trade?"

"One silver for twenty-five coppers," Sarita offered.

"They're only ten-"

"Valley-man silver, not galactic," she clarified. "Twenty-five plus an off-record phone call."

The panel shut, and there was some activity behind the door. It slid open again. "Among asteroids or beyond the thirty-three?"

"Local."

"Twenty-three coppers and a free phone call, unlimited reasonable time."

"Agreed," she said.

"Enter." The doors opened to a dark, messy room, a girthy woman on the other side, tapping her foot impatiently.

Sarita held out the silver, and the woman quickly snatched it out of her hand. "No refunds." She pointed to the computer at the far end, while dropping twenty-three copper discs into my hand.

After some poking and patience, the screen on the older green brick displayed the word "Calling." After a few moments, a click was heard from the other end of the call, and a male voice said, "Khani Kamadara, Second in Command, here answering for the Valley Chief. Leave a message."

She recognized the voice. "Chaha and the medicine are missing. I'm guessing that she took some medicine to find you," Sarita said.

"Chaha's missing?" he shouted.

"The medicine was not originally planned to be sent down till after the upcoming blizzard. She might have heard the argument like half the compound did and decided to take matters into her own hands," she said.

"We need that medicine!" Khani said. "The metals, especially the silver veins, release a chilling energy. It can give us fatal frostbite. If that wasn't bad enough, the latest explosion had a nasty pathogen in it, unlike anything we have seen before. The ice punctured our mining gear, and the slime is rotting our blood. It's being passed through coughing so quickly that those who tend the sick become the sick. If we don't get that blood-making, purifying medicine in our healing pods within the next day, at least a third of us will die. Most of us want to see Chaha again. Oh, poor Chaha. I hope she is still alive."

"Granny hated her for some reason. Following the crowd is too easy when she can control the contracts. But sometimes, siding with you has its perks," Sarita said, holding up some coins.

"I will keep that in mind while I get a search party ready. Almost everyone who isn't sick with shiver-blight is busy caring for the rest. But for the patriarch's daughter, we will find her," said Khani.

Ninth Step Down

CHAHA

I was still kneeling, trying to beat the ice sheet with rocks to no avail. Just hurting my hands. Desperate, I tried something else that I hoped would work.

Recalling my lessons, I breathed in and felt the heat in my chest and said, "Pānī ra hāvā paglanuhōs. Melt water and wind." And nothing. The only thing that moved was not the ice, but the roars coming closer.

"I'm a failure, and I'm going to die because I can never summon a stupid snowflake," I said miserably. Another roar thundered in the air, ever closer now.

The anger and frustration welled up inside me, and I slammed my fists into the ice. The heat in my chest flowed into my arms and my hands. The ice began to hiss, as if hot metal was cutting through it. As if I was getting free.

"Wait, no... maybe, maybe I will never have the powers of ice." I could feel my entire body growing a little bit warmer. "Maybe, I can have fire. Fire!"

I slammed my fists into the ice, and the water hissed and bubbled. Punch after punch, strike after strike, the thick ice melted away, and in moments, my fist punched through to the outside world. In just a few more moments, the fist-sized hole became large enough to crawl through. Looking over my left shoulder, I saw shaking, quivering, rippling fur rushing toward me.

I had to take a chance. With a full-body tackle, carrying the pack on my back, I somehow slid through the opening. It was wet, cold, and safe. "It's the path!" I screamed. "Beards, here I come!"

A hungry, brutal roar behind me made me twist and fall. The one-eyed bear, with most of its snout melted off, loomed on the other side of the hole in the ice. A mix of its own blood and familiar fur speckled the scarred area.

"You, you ate Huggy," I said sadly. Without realizing it, I had named the sloth.

The bear kept trying to push its entire body through the ice sheet to get out of the hole to eat me. I turned to run, moving as fast as my legs would carry me. The ice straining and cracking behind me, I wished the Beards were with me, that they would help me. I tried to feel the heat again, and I felt sparks flaring up, burning my body, so I had to stop.

Then a familiar warm, gentle heat encompassed me along with my happy memories with the Beards. I heard Leader Beard's voice as if were whispering in my ear.

"Bears are dangerous, especially the snow sloth bears, and they're faster than they look. Weave between trees or bring a massive gun. Only a predator has a chance at fighting another predator." He had then tapped his long-barreled rifle.

I ran between the thick cedar, chir, and blue pines. I heard a great crack and the sound of something shattering, then the bear began to chase me in earnest. Thankfully, the trees were getting thicker, so I ran to the left, then swerved to the right. The bear had to slow down to go around each tree. Yet every time I looked behind me, it drew closer and closer.

My head whipping around, I could see the village of the Beards. I was getting closer, but the bear was faster than me. Out of the corner of my eye, I saw birds flying. Pheasants may be out and about, finding more food. Or maybe running from something.

Before I could think it through, I turned and ran toward the Monal Pheasants. They changed their direction to fly away from me. I heard the growl and hiss of a predator cat. A Siberian sabertooth was trying to hunt them down. Clearly thinking me the easier prey, it now started chasing me.

I tried to keep running but tripped on a root and tumbled. Curling up to protect my head, I thought, *Is this how I die, because of shoddy boots?*

The tiger roared, and the bear growled, and I expected to be torn apart by monsters. Instead, the snow-sloth bear and the Siberian saber-toothed tiger turned to face each other. I realized the bear was hungry, and the tiger was territorial. Neither one could back down; they had to fight.

I got up and started running again, looking back only once to see the two claw, bite, rip, and tear into each other. I was not sticking around to see who won.

Especially since I could see the path.

My lungs burned, and my legs were heavy, so I had to slow to a walk. The village was so close, and the wind was picking up. Not just loose snowflakes, but the start of a blizzard. One flake became ten, a hundred, thousands, then billions. And yet I could see the village. Amidst the whipping winds, the light-gray and brown buildings were covered in colorful red, blue, and yellow patterns.

"Just like their clothes. Simple, yet colorful," I said with a smile. The village looked better than I'd imagined. The stonework was so smooth that it looked like the refined metal of spaceships. Each house looked like a smooth painted boulder carved out of the mountain yet also looked as if it would fly into space.

The sun was threatening to set when I came to a narrow path. Steep sides, covered in creeping frostbite vines forced me to cross a bridge even though a large herd of goats were in the way. "No turning back now," I said to the goat herd. As I approached the bridge and the goats who looked like walking snowdrifts, one came to me. The leader of the goat herd brayed and screamed. But this was no monster; it was an animal.

So, I knelt, grabbed some of the moss nearby, and with a solid tug, tore it free. I could feel a tiny bit of heat as if I were going to have a memory, but instead it went into the moss. The moss became warm, instantly melting the snow and water on it. I offered the warmed moss to the animal. The leader goat stopped braying, sniffed the offering, then ate it out of my hand. It then turned to the herd, and with a scream, walked to the village. The goat herd parted and let me walk through.

On the other side of the goat herd, I heard someone scream, "Chaha!" Looking up, I saw it was Second Beard, his face a mix of fear and wonder. That was the first time I'd ever seen him scared.

He ran and picked me up, tattered bag and all, and gave me a massive hug. "Chaha, I just got the call. How?! Why? How could you?" His hug only grew tighter and warmer, and his heat radiated out, melting and drying the snow and water on my clothes. I hugged back and felt a tinge of my own fire meet his.

That's when I closed my eyes and fell into the void.

Tenth Step Down

KHANI

As second in command of the mining company, I, Khani Kamadara, was not having a good day. While another one of my crew was dying, I was interrupted by a call. I picked it up, hoping it was good news.

Instead, Chaha, the leader's daughter, the last gift his wife gave him, was missing. He was miserable to be around for a year after his wife's passing, and I don't want to find out what his mourning period for Chaha would be. So, I took three men and we each went to different entry points of the village to operate drones.

I was on my way to collect some spare drones when I experienced miracles.

First, Chaha was alive. Despite this weather, the animals, and the distance. Second, she emerged not from the rails but from the walking trail.

Third, the onerous goats that tackled everything were giving her space to walk. Fourth, Brownie the Terai goat, the unmanageable leader, was leading her to us.

Fifth, when I picked her up, I could feel enough heat from the medicine to save us all. Sixth, when I tried to use my power to warm her up, I felt my power meet a new heat.

Seventh, she passed out in my arms, drifting to sleep.

I could be shocked later, but right now, I can't let her sacrifice be in vain. Pressing the button on my coms, I said, "Chaha made it down the mountain! Come back from your posts and get everyone in the med pods now!"

The next several hours were spent grabbing people, stripping them of clothes, and putting them in the pods. Without the primary liquid medicine, the pods were nothing more than airtight coffins. With the L.A.V.A. serum—a mix of artificial stem cells, restorative proteins, and a bunch of other stuff—the pods become lifesavers. Frostbitten tissue dissolved and restored. Mucus-filled lungs? Really bad hangovers? A few drops, an hour-long dunk, and you're back to yourself. I'm glad I paid attention when our medic was rambling. It made helping others, and now Chaha, much easier.

When I took her clothes off to put her in the pod, my hands started to shake. Scratches and bruises were swelling up all over her body. Parts of her toes and fingers were discolored. Frostbite. Even on men, it's hard to see. But on a twelve-year-old girl?

I put her carefully in the pod and turned it on. The machine beeped and strapped her down to the table. The casing sealed up, and fluid-like blood and regenerative fluid as blue as the sky flooded in, beginning the healing process. On the capsule's screen, all sorts of info was displayed, but at the top left it said, "Estimated Healing Time: Unknown."

Less than an hour later, once the sick were in the healing pods, I went to our crew and said, "Everyone, you need to know this about Chaha. When I put her in the capsule, the estimated time was unknown."

You could hear a snowflake drop. We all knew what that meant.

LEADER BEARD

Up on the mountain, I got a call from Khani as I was departing.

He told me, "Boss, Chaha made it down here, she is still alive and brought enough L.A.V.A that we and she will be safe. Not only that, but her pod says the recovery time is unknown. And I also got some camera footage from a building that you'll want to see. Show this to the matriarch."

Granny and I watched the footage on the coms together. The snow somewhat obscured what was happening, but Chaha was clearly doing something to the moss to warm it. The orange light over the moss was unmistakable.

The matriarch felt shock spread throughout her entire body. "How, how is that possible? That should be impossible. Getting the injection that allows women to use ice and men to use fire makes you sterile for a year. And no woman can do fire." She stared at me. "My daughter and you disappeared for a year, and you came back with a brat and my daughter's corpse," she said.

"She froze some of her eggs before she got the injection. So, when we left for that trip, she got some of them back, and we conceived on our elopement night. When we tried to have the baby, something was wrong. The only message we received from the birthing pod was 'incompatible blood.' I had to choose who to save. She rubbed her belly with a smile every day. She would have never forgiven me if I'd put her over the child, our Chaha." I shook my head. "Did you not read any of my letters? My messages?"

Granny had no words. Confusion and shock still overtook her mind.

I said, "She is your granddaughter. And yes, I am aware that this would make her the first female with fire. It's hard to believe. From what the medic can figure out, because Chaha was conceived with eggs created before her mother's injection, it gave Chaha the chance to inherit my power. Maybe you can now believe I'm not a scoundrel that kidnaps children. She is mine, and she is ours. And you and I both know that if the estimated time of healing is unknown, there is a serious chance that she may die. If she lives, she needs to be treated better. By her whole family."

Granny, looking so old and almost regretful, said, "Well, if she is my grand-daughter, she can be moved to another room. Maybe one farther down the mountain."

"I can work with that."

CHAHA

As I started to wake up, I realized I was in a capsule, strapped down and covered in reddish orange and light-blue liquid. The lid popped open, the side bent out, and the restraints snapped off, letting me stumble out. I was alone in the room.

"Wait, the medicine?" I jerked my head back and forth frantically until I saw one of the capsules in the pod, almost empty, but still in the machine. *I made it!*

Nearby was a shower space. I entered it and turned the water temperature to hot. The sticky fluid was absorbed by my skin as much as it was washed off. Drying off with a nearby towel,

I dressed in warm, fitting shoes and soft, casual clothes.

I made my way to the door and read the posted note out loud. "Chaha, when you wake up, please take a shower and find some clothes on the table. When you're ready, go through the doors then down the hall to the right."

Shoving them open tore the note in half, and all surrounding noise went quiet. I kept walking, no longer on a rocky path, but on a floor, my boots making a tapping sound. Down the hall, I turned the corner and found myself in a large room.

Leader Beard, the matriarch, numerous other Beards, and even a few teachers and classmates were waiting. Leader Beard ran to me and picked me up in a hug. The whole room of people came to me, and the entire room turned into one enormous hug.

Leader Beard said, "Chaha, everyone is safe because of you. Thank you. And I can finally say it. I can finally say that I'm your father. We can finally be together!"

"Father?" I said softly.

The warmth and the gentle pressure were too much for me. I started crying. All the struggles I'd experienced finally seemed to leave me with each teardrop. The candy, the head pats, the books, and all the little bits of advice clicked. It made sense.

For the first time in a long time, I was happy—finally with friends and family.

Epilogue

Far from Chaha and her now larger family, a weakened Elder Glass Lava Goop fought a demon of winds and frostbite, a little bringer of despair and death.

The demon and goop grew weaker and weaker, trading blows and strikes, wind and glass, living fire and dead wind.

"Stubborn fool. All you protect is meaningless," the demon taunted. "Everything shall perish, everything shall return to the void. That light you all are hoping for shall not descend. There is only us. I force you to wither and shake off your very presence. And now that there is so little of you left, it's time for all your glass to finally cool off."

The demonic presence, though severely weakened, turned into a great wind, with asymmetrical, jagged barbs of numbing exhaustion. It began to blow and heave about, swirling all over the diminishing, transparent lava. It let loose a cry of beeps and bubbles— pain from the fight and this attack. The entire surface of the goop became solid, cold, and dead. The wind pressed harder into the goop, trying to whip and tear away until there was nothing left.

Both were diminishing. The demon's wind was like a mountain blizzard blowing against a cracking, splitting, shattering boulder, wearing it down to a lump no bigger than a human. The demonic wind was far larger and greater.

"You may have saved these stories, but you won't live to save another! I will still linger on after beating you, and the heroes that may be, never shall be! More of existence shall turn to oblivion, as my frostbite numbs hands, heads, and hearts. You die for nothing!" The malice-filled cackling laughter echoed.

The goop made a single glass-cracking sound. The hardened exterior was not sloughed off this time but pulled into itself. It was being used as fuel. And the glass burned hotter, brighter. The molten glass jutted out in perfect symmetry, a mix of flowing fractals and runny droplets like a spiked ball. With all the wind flowing so close to its skin, it could not move away from the spikes, each one stabbing, carving, cutting, and dripping into every part of the wind.

The worst part for the demon?

The hope, the joy, that warmth that coated every bit of its presence dissolving it away into something—not nothingness. Not a void.

Experience. Fuel for the Elder Glass Lava Goop. It was absorbing the wind, the numbing despair, and using it to burn brighter, hotter than ever before in the fight.

All that fighting and the demon only facilitated what it hated. It gave one last howl and withered away, the last of its presence falling deep into the great Shadow of Despair, where all demons dwell.

The elder, once as large as a volcanic explosion, was now so small and weakened, with the same coloration as L.A.V.A., but hotter, purer, and more vibrant.

So it went back to its home, far from the coldest reaches of Wisdom's Waters, and went on to where the water flowed freely into count-less streams alongside Fanatic Fires, which burned without consumption and warmed some streams into steam and others into boiling tendrils. In this great central region of heat, the goop saw friends, old and freshly hatched.

Some spoke with words, others with gurgles and slaps. Some put their thought out for all to experience, and others remained silent, resonating with the crowds. The goop rested by allies and friends, clanking metal, thriving boulders, puddles with three mouths and six eyes, and a tall chir pine, dancing with every branch and root. It was surrounded by so many other goops that it was now okay for the elder to rest.

The story was saved, and it even became something more.

Glossary

Note: Nepalese words use a writing system with no easy translation to English writing. So, the closest approximate word sounds have been used for a reader's ease and delight.

batāsakō: Nepalese for wind.

chyangra: Nepalese word specifically referring to goats that are usually white with long, thick fur, and that can be wild or domesticated and live high in the mountains.

Elder: Highest rank for women on Frostfire Asteroid 12. Don't have to prepare teaching plans. Handle building repairs, manage food, do paperwork, and more.

Fanatic Fires: One of the great domains between and foundational to the existence of space and time. From this place, all fire, heat, passion, intense emotions, new ideas, and mental refinement flow out into adjoining realms and dimensions that are influenced by space and time.

Grand Elder: Head of the Elders, always a woman, paid the most, and willing to do more work in a day than anyone else, every day.

khana: Nepalese word roughly meaning meal or food, but also to eat.

pānī: Nepalese for water.

pānī ra batāsakō sātha, ēka kama uṭhnuhōs: One of the spells that Nepalese women can use after being injected with a special light-blue concoction. It translates to something like "water and wind, rise-move figure."

pānī ra batāsakō sātha, rahanuhōs: One of the spells that Nepalese women can use after being injected with a special light-blue colored concoction. It translates to something like "water and wind, catch person."

ra: conjunction in Nepalese "and."

Shadow(s) of Despair: One of the great domains between and foundational to the existence of space and time. This was once the great place of shadows of confusion and be-wilderment, where shadows danced amid mysteries and chaotic opportunities. Now, it is the haunt of demons, who gather together.

Solid waters: What if water were hard, but not cold? What would warm or hot solid water feel like? This impossibility is solid water.

Star of Nepal: The first age of mass space exploration began after 3000. Some Nepalese went off to form a daughter city called Star of Nepal. The claimed area expanded, which is collectively called New Nepal. At the time of this tale, this territory included some of the Frostfire asteroids.

Talking boxes: Galactic communication computers.

Teacher: Manages and teaches the classmates. Rank below the Elders.

terai - Nepalese word referring to goats that are dark brown with some white coloring, short hair, and commonly raised in the lower plain and valley regions.

Waters of Wisdom: One of the great domains between and foundational to the existence of space and time. From this place, all liquids and fluids cascade out into adjoining realms and dimensions that are influenced by space and time. This includes the flow of thoughts, the feeling of time flowing by, the erosion of ignorance, and how wisdom drenches mortals.

Afterword

Thank you for reading this work. While I was earning my Master of Science in Plant Science, I had the pleasure of meeting several Nepalese people, and I knew I wanted to create something interesting inspired by their culture and ecosystem. Much of this work is rooted in existing terrain, plants, animals, and more. It's supported not just by research but by the stories they tell. This may not be the most accurate, factual work, but I believe the vibes and the essence of never giving up are well showcased.

One person told me about four indigenous goat breeds found in Nepal. The Chyangras are white with thick, long fur and raised in the high mountains. They can go wild fast and become quite the menace. Sinhals are usually white, but sometimes have reddish-brown faces and spots, and are found in the high hills and low mountain regions. Kharis tend to be lighter brown and are raised in the hilly areas. Terais tend to be a darker brown with some white coloring and are commonly raised in the lower plain regions of the country.

As a botanist, hearing stories from peers involving local, native plants was cool. Rhododendrons were a particular favorite flower for their color and hardiness. Trees such as deodar cedars, chir pines, blue pines, and morinda spruce were common and essential to their way of life. Some of my peers were more suburban and enjoyed the sights. Others were from the rugged countryside and had to work the wood to make tool handles, burn the leaves for rituals, and make use of them in other ways.

One of the ladies described some interesting butterflies, which I later found out were great mormons and common brimstones. She led me down a rabbit hole that helped me learn about Monal Pheasants too.

Interesting conversations were heard in the office. One of them was a debate over which mammal in Nepal was the meanest, excluding humans, of course. That's how I found out about sloth bears.

Sometimes the homesick Nepalese would talk about food they missed: momo dumplings, thukpa noodle soup, sel roti bread, and chatamari. They spoke of these foods like Americans talk about missing burgers, pizza, PB&Js, and s'mores on holiday trips.

My personal interest in fossils helped me add a few more animals to the mix. Saber-toothed tigers never get enough love.

I personally hate the cold. Snowstorms feel like frostbite weather, and it kills my plants. So, writing about a little girl overcoming blizzard conditions felt like overcoming my own issues with cold.

If you are interested in reading more of my work, feel free to visit my website:

www.jjbartel.com

If you want to receive occasional updates and early sneak peeks at some of my writings, subscribe to my page at SubscribeStar:

www.subscribestar.com/j-j-bartel

About the Author

J. J. Bartel is an author, botanist, historian, and gamer. He has written and told stories from a young age. Topics that his novels and short stories focus on include plants, botany, history, theology, fantasy, comedy, horror, and science fiction. He earned a Bachelor of Science in Biology, a Bachelor of Arts in History, and a Biotechnology Certificate from Northern State University, as well as a Master of Science in Plant Science from South Dakota State University. Currently, he is in the process of publishing multiple books and doing home garden experiments. He works as an analytical researcher and university instructor.